Cricket's Song

Written by
Bing Bo

Illustrated by
Xing Huo

CARDINAL
MEDIA

Fern lived in a little cottage
in the forest.

One summer morning she heard
music outside her window.

She searched for the sound and
found Cricket hiding in the leaves.

Fern picked him up gently and he brushed his antennae over her cheek. It was his way of saying hello.

It began to rain, so Fern set Cricket beneath a branch. His friends Grasshopper and Firefly joined him.

Fern said, "I will make a little house to protect you."

Fern wove twigs and leaves into a cozy house for her new forest friends.

Cricket brushed his long antennae
over Fern's cheek. It was his way of
saying thank you.

"Hey, that tickles!" she laughed.
"Now go inside."

Grasshopper jumped into the house. Firefly zoomed in to join her. Cricket began to play his music to the rhythm of the raindrops.

The world outside was soaked.
But inside the house, everyone
was warm and dry.

Each morning Cricket would sit
under Fern's window and play a
song to wake her. Each morning
his music was the first thing Fern
heard as she opened her eyes.

When summer turned to fall, Cricket's music was harder to hear through Fern's closed windows. Fern would listen closely each morning until she heard his song.

Winter arrived suddenly. Cricket tried to wake Fern with his music, but he was too cold to go under her window.

When Fern woke to silence, she opened her bedroom window and gasped at the snow!

She ran to the little house and looked inside. Cricket, Grasshopper, and Firefly huddled together to stay warm.

Cricket brushed his long antennae over Fern's cheek. It was his way of saying goodbye.

"I will miss your song," Fern told him, "but I will come back in the spring."

After winter passed, Fern visited the tree house.

Out of the tiny door rushed little crickets, grasshoppers, and fireflies! One cricket brushed his antennae on her. It was his way of saying hello.

Fern laughed and thought how wonderful it would be to hear a song outside her window again.

Text Copyright © Bing Bo
Illustration Copyright © Xing Huo
Edited by Karen Wendlandt
English Copyright © 2018 by Cardinal Media, LLC.

ISBN 978-1-64074-027-3

Printed in China
2 4 6 8 10 9 7 5 3 1